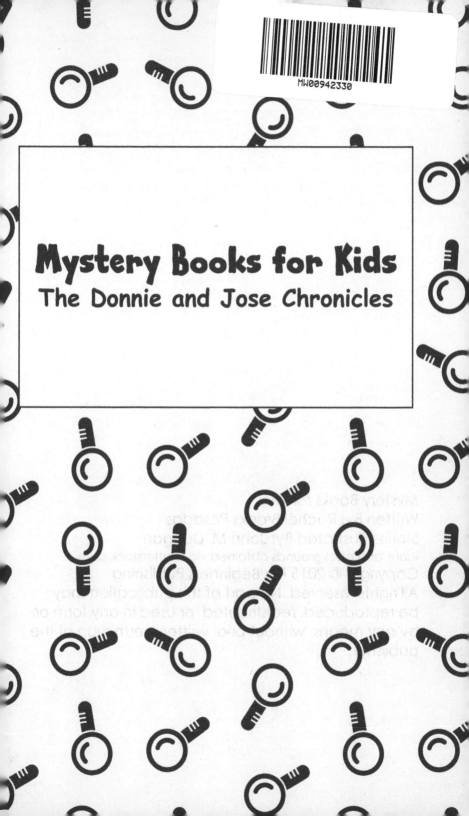

Mystery Books for Kids
The Donnie and Jose Chronicles

Mystery Books for Kids
Written By: Rachel Brooks Posadas
Stories Illustrated By: John M. Duggan
Icons and backgrounds obtained via Shutterstock.com
Copyright © 2015 For Beginners Publishing

Table of Contents

Mystery of the
Broken Windows

Donnie gazed out the window as the school bus slowly bumped along. The cloudy day matched his unhappy mood. He couldn't believe his bad luck that morning.

The bus stopped to collect the last batch of kids before arriving at school.

"Hey, Donnie," said Jose as he slid into the seat next to Donnie. He was holding a huge cinnamon roll wrapped in a napkin. "Want some?"

"No thanks. I already ate," said Donnie. "You're not going to believe what happened this morning."

"What happened?" Jose asked with a mouth full of cinnamon roll.

"I got grounded," explained Donnie. "My neighbor Mrs. Whitmore thinks I broke her window."

"Did you?" Jose asked.

"No!" Donnie snapped. "Someone threw a rock through her kitchen window this morning, and she thinks it was me because I was out walking my dog around that time."

"Sorry, Donnie. That's rough," sympathized Jose. "Who do you think really broke it?"

"I don't know, but I'm going to find out," answered Donnie.

Donnie enjoyed school most days. But that day seemed endless. He didn't even have much fun during gym when they played his favorite game: kickball. He couldn't stop thinking about the broken window. He didn't like being blamed for something he didn't do and was determined to get to the bottom of this mystery.

On the bus ride home, with his thick blue notebook open on his lap and a pencil stub tucked above his ear, Donnie got to work.

"What are you doing?" asked Jose.

"I'm making a list of everyone who was outside early enough to have broken that window," Donnie responded.

"Cool! Can I help?" asked Jose.

"Sure," said Donnie.

"Who do you have so far?" Jose asked curiously.

"Well, since it happened around the time I was walking Bessie, it couldn't have been anyone who was already gone for work," explained Donnie. "That leaves everyone home getting ready for school. But I doubt it was any of the kids our age. I never see any of them out that early. But sometimes I do see their older brothers and sisters who are all in high school."

"How many are there?" asked Jose.

"Three," answered Donnie. "Lisa Reynolds, Ricky Smizer, and Greg Whitmore."

"Greg Whitmore?" Jose questioned Donnie. "You think he broke his own window?"

"I don't know. Maybe," said Donnie. "Maybe not. I doubt it was Lisa either. But everyone knows what a bully Ricky is, and he's at the top of my list."

"Do you want me to come over and help you investigate?" Jose offered.

"Not today. My mom won't let anyone come over since I'm grounded," Donnie replied. "Besides, I'll have to wait until morning when

I walk Bessie to search for clues."

"Alright, see you tomorrow then," Jose waved goodbye and prepared to get off the bus as it approached his stop.

The next morning, Donnie was up and out the door earlier than usual to walk Bessie. He wanted to look around the neighborhood for clues, and the first place he wanted to start was with the rock that had broken the Whitmore window. If he could match it to the rocks in someone's yard or garden, that person might be the window breaker. There was just one problem, though. He was too nervous to ask Mrs. Whitmore if he could see the rock. She still thought he was the guilty one.

As he approached the Whitmore house, a commotion at the end of the block caught his attention. Old man Farley was standing in his front yard with another neighbor. Donnie couldn't make out what they were saying

exactly, but Farley definitely sounded angry. He'd even taken off the brown safari hat he always wore while working in his yard and garden and was waving it around with his hands up in the air. Bessie stopped to sniff around the base of a big oak tree, but Donnie nudged her forward. He had to find out what was happening at Farley's.

As Donnie approached Farley's house, he finally understood why the old man was so angry. And he couldn't believe it. Right there on the front of the old man's house was a broken window, just like the Whitmore house.

Donnie suddenly felt nervous and wanted to turn around and head home before Farley spotted him. But his curiosity wouldn't let him leave just yet. This was his chance to ask some questions and figure out who was breaking windows in the neighborhood. Before Donnie could ask any questions, though, Mr. Farley had one for him.

"Hey, you there! Aren't you the kid who broke Mrs. Whitmore's window?" Farley said in a gruff voice. "I know you broke my window too!"

"N-n-no," stammered Donnie. "It wasn't me."

"Which house is yours? I want to talk to your parents," declared Farley.

"But I didn't do anything," insisted Donnie.

Bessie started barking again, which only irritated old man Farley.

"Keep your dog off my lawn and away from my flowers. I just planted these! You kids are always messing up my yard," yelled Farley. "Go on now. Get your dog out of here. You can bet I'll be talking to your parents soon.

Donnie spun around quickly, ready to run home. But he didn't get far. He had only taken a few steps when he ran smack into Ricky Smizer. Ricky was fifteen and had a reputation for causing trouble. He seemed especially fond of picking on younger kids. Donnie was afraid of Ricky and avoided him as much as possible.

"Watch where you're going!" Ricky shouted at Donnie. "Next time I'll punch your lights out."

***

Donnie and Jose pushed their empty trays along the metal counter as they waited in the lunch line to receive a giant slice of cheese or pepperoni pizza.

"I'm starving," announced Jose. "I hope they don't run out of pepperoni before we get up there. Plain cheese just isn't as good."

Jose was still talking about the pizza when Donnie interrupted. "Hey, did I tell you that another window was broken this morning?"

"No way!" Jose exclaimed. "This is getting weird."

"Remember that cranky old man at the end

of the block?" said Donnie.

"You mean the one who always yells at everyone to stay off his lawn?" Jose asked.

"Yep, that's the guy," answered Donnie. "This time it was his house."

"So you still think it was Ricky?" asked Jose.

"Now, I definitely think it was Ricky," Donnie replied.

The boys pushed their trays closer to the front of the pizza line. The aroma of piping-hot pepperoni wafted their way.

"Mm, that smells good," said Jose.

"Old man Farley is always yelling at Ricky and the other teens for cutting across his yard on the way to school," explained Donnie. "He really gets under Ricky's skin. I wouldn't be surprised if Ricky just wanted to get him back."

"Yes! There's still pepperoni pizza," Jose said excitedly.

Since Donnie was still grounded, his only chance to look for clues around the neighborhood was before school during Bessie's morning walk. But this time he didn't want Bessie barking and ruining his chance to investigate.

"I'm sorry, Bessie. You have to wait here today," Donnie apologized as he tied her leash to his old swing set in the backyard. "I'll be back in a few minutes, girl. There's something I have to do."

Donnie had a plan. He would wait outside Ricky Smizer's house. It was the biggest house on the block, home to the neighborhood bully. Donnie just hoped he wouldn't get beaten up by Ricky if he got caught spying on him.

A row of tall bushes lined one side of Ricky's front yard between his house and the neighbor's. It was a perfect hiding spot. Donnie crouched down beneath the bushes and waited. He was ready to catch Ricky breaking another window. But Donnie was so focused on staring at Ricky's front door, waiting for him to come out, that he didn't notice someone coming up behind him.

"So you're the one breaking all these windows," a familiar voice shouted just as someone grabbed the back of Donnie's shirt and pulled him up from the ground. It was Ricky Smizer. Donnie knew he was in trouble.

"Well, what do you know? Someone just broke a window on the side of my house and here you are hiding in the bushes," snarled Ricky. "Looks like you finally got caught, kid."

"No, it wasn't me Ricky," said Donnie. "I was trying to catch you breaking another window."

"Oh, so you're spying on me?" accused Ricky. "Give me one good reason why I shouldn't pound you right now, kid."

"I'm telling the truth. I swear I didn't do it, but you can help me find out who

did." Donnie's hands were shaking, and he felt nervous. If only Ricky would believe him.

Ricky stood quietly, thinking for a minute. Donnie couldn't take the suspense. The next moment could either mean relief if Ricky believed him or a punch in the face if he didn't.

"Alright. Come on, kid. Let's go look at the window. If there's any sign that someone else broke it, you're off the hook – for now." With that, Ricky led the way toward the other side of his house where a small window near the back door had been shattered.

Ricky examined some shards of glass that had fallen on the window sill. Donnie inspected the ground below.

"Hey! I think I found a footprint," Donnie exclaimed excitedly.

"Let me see," said Ricky. He stood over the footprint peering down at it for a minute. Then, carefully, he placed his foot right next to the footprint. The print was fresh and just slightly larger than Ricky's shoe. "This is a man's shoe print," he said. "It's definitely too big to be yours. Someone else was just here."

"Well, it looks like whoever left it headed through your backyard," Donnie observed.

Ricky nodded in agreement. "We can't do much about it now, kid. I gotta go. Can't be late to school again or I'll get suspended," answered Ricky. "Meet me in front of my house early tomorrow morning. We're gonna catch this window breaker once and for all. And when we do..." An angry look came over Ricky's face, and he didn't finish what he was saying.

Donnie ran home. He had to get Bessie from the backyard; then catch the bus to school. He could barely wait for tomorrow morning when he might finally discover the true identity of the window breaker.

"Psst. Psst. Jose," whispered Donnie.

Jose had missed the bus that morning and his older brother had dropped him off so Donnie never got to tell him about the latest development with the broken windows in his neighborhood. Donnie just couldn't wait until lunch to tell Jose about all the excitement that morning with Ricky.

"Jose," Donnie whispered again.

"Shh. You're going to get us in trouble, Donnie," warned Jose.

"But you won't believe what happened," Donnie continued. "Ricky didn't do it. And he's going to help me find out who did."

"Didn't do what?" asked Jose.

"Break the windows," Donnie answered. "He's not the one breaking windows."

"Oh. Well, tell me about it at lunch," suggested Jose. "You know today is cheeseburgers. I can't wait."

Jose might have been more interested in cheeseburgers right then, but Donnie was focused on solving his little mystery. It was just too bad he'd have to wait until morning to do so.

**

Donnie felt bad leaving Bessie behind again the following morning, but he had a mystery to solve. He rushed down the block to Ricky's house. Ricky was already waiting outside. He gave a quick nod hello as Donnie approached.

"Hey, Ricky," Donnie greeted him excitedly. "Where should we start?"

"Shh," Ricky held an index finger up to his lips and pointed toward the house next door. It was Lisa Reynold's house, one of the other teenagers in the neighborhood. Donnie glanced over, but didn't see anyone. Ricky motioned to duck down behind the bushes. Donnie ducked down, but poked his head up for a quick peek.

Just then, they heard shattering glass and a loud thud. Another window had been broken! Ricky darted toward the noise. Donnie ran after him, but couldn't keep up. Ricky was too fast. As Donnie came around the back of the neighbor's house, he saw a hooded figure slip out the back gate with Ricky close behind. Donnie sprinted toward them.

When Donnie finally caught up with Ricky, he couldn't believe his eyes. The hooded figure was none other than old man Farley. Ricky was arguing with him. The two were yelling back and forth loud enough for half the block to hear, and soon, neighbors emerged from their homes and began gathering around. Once Farley noticed the crowd, he got quiet.

"Can you guys believe old man Farley's the one breaking all the windows?" Ricky announced to the crowd. "Let's see. First, you

broke Greg's window, then mine, and now Lisa's. Why are you targeting all the teens?"

Farley didn't answer.

"Wait," Donnie interrupted. "It doesn't make any sense. Mr. Farley's window got broken too. Why would he do that?"

Everyone was quiet, waiting for Farley to respond. A few minutes ticked by without Farley saying a word. He was staring down at his dirt-smudged, green gardening boots.

"Come on, Farley. Say something," prodded a voice from the crowd.

Farley cleared his throat and looked up at everyone circled around him. He took a slow, deep breath.

"Okay, I did it," confessed Farley. "I broke the windows."

"But why?" asked Donnie.

"I work so hard on my lawn and my little flower

garden, and those careless teens are always cutting across my yard," explained Farley. "Do you know how many times I've had to replant grass seed or nurse my flowers back to good health because those three kids are always stepping on something every day?"

Ricky spoke up and apologized. "We're sorry, Mr. Farley. We never meant to ruin your plants. We were just cutting through your yard on the way to school. We'll be more careful now."

"Hold on," said Donnie. "Why would you break your own window, Mr. Farley?"

"Well, I didn't want anyone to know it was me breaking the windows, so I threw a rock through my own window. Who would suspect me of breaking my own window?" explained Farley.

Everyone stood around discussing this sudden turn of events a bit longer. Farley promised to pay for all the broken windows, and the teens promised to stop cutting through his yard.

Donnie left them all behind as they continued talking. He felt bad for leaving Bessie home and wanted to give her a quick walk. Plus, who knows what other mystery he might encounter on another walk through the neighborhood.

Case of the Missing Art Supplies

D onnie and Jose were stuck at the end of a long line in the cafeteria.

"Why is it taking so long?" Jose complained. "They must have run out of the chicken strips and have to make more. Everybody likes those."

"Oh, no," Donnie sighed. "I forgot my lunch ticket in my desk. I'll be right back. Maybe Miss Gruber's still in the classroom so I can get it."

Donnie hustled back to class. His sneakers kept squeaking across the shiny linoleum floor as he sprinted through the halls. Just as he was about to turn the corner to the fourth-grade hallway, he bumped into Maribel, one of the fifth graders.

"Oops, sorry," Donnie apologized.

"That's okay, it's my fault," insisted Maribel. "I was in a hurry. I guess that's one reason they're always telling us not to run in the halls." She and Donnie both laughed. "See you later."

Donnie nodded and continued down the hallway to his fourth-grade classroom. He peeked through the rectangular window in the door, but didn't see Miss Gruber. She must have already gone to lunch. Donnie slid down to the floor and sat with his back against the door. What was he going to do now?

"Hey there, what's the matter?" asked a gentle voice.

Donnie looked up. It was Carl, the school janitor. In one hand, he held the wooden

handle of the big, wide sweeper he used for dusting the hallway floors during the day. In the other hand jangled the huge ring of keys he always carried.

"I forgot my lunch ticket in my desk, and my teacher isn't in there anymore," explained Donnie.

"Well, I'm sure I can help with that," Carl said with a smile. "Now, let me see. Which key is it?" He fumbled through the keys for a moment. "This ought to be it."

Carl turned a key in the lock, but it got stuck. He grabbed hold of the door knob with one hand as he tried wiggling out the stuck key with the other. When he did that, the key came loose, and the door opened.

"Looks like the door was already unlocked," Carl said, surprised. "Well, hurry and get your lunch ticket. Don't worry about the door. I'll be back to lock it in a minute," Carl assured as he continued sweeping where he'd left off.

Donnie searched his desk for his lunch ticket, but couldn't find it. He looked around the classroom, trying to remember if he had set it down somewhere else before washing his hands for lunch. He didn't see his ticket anywhere, but made another discovery instead.

The cabinet where Miss Gruber kept all the art supplies was wide open and completely empty. Donnie thought she'd said they wouldn't be making the art project for the parents' open house until next week. Maybe she changed her mind.

"Donnie, what are you doing back here? You should be at lunch," the unexpected sound of Miss Gruber's voice took Donnie by surprise.

"I can't find my lunch ticket," explained Donnie. "Wait a second." Donnie reached into his back pocket and there it was...his lunch ticket.

"What happened here?" asked Miss Gruber looking at the empty art supplies cabinet.

"It was like that when I came in," said Donnie.

"Donnie, I want you to tell me the truth now," Miss Gruber said sternly. "Did you take the art supplies out of the cabinet?"

"What? No," said Donnie.

"Donnie, if I find any of the art supplies in your desk or locker you know I'm going to have to send you to the principal's office and call your mom." Miss Gruber sounded disappointed.

"But I didn't take anything," Donnie insisted.

"You better get to lunch before you miss it," said Miss Gruber. "Go on. We'll talk more about this later."

Jose was already eating his chicken strips and tater tots when Donnie got back to the noisy lunchroom. There was no line now. Everyone was already eating, so Donnie quickly grabbed his tray of food and sat down next to Jose.

"What took you so long?" asked Jose, still chewing on a tater tot.

"I've got another mystery to solve!" exclaimed Donnie.

"What happened now?" Jose asked.

"All the art supplies Miss Gruber brought in are missing," Donnie explained. "Now, we have nothing to make for the open house next week. And worse than that, she thinks I took the supplies."

"Wow. I'm glad I'm not you, Donnie. You're always a suspect," Jose joked and both boys smiled. "But seriously, I wonder who did take the supplies?" pondered Jose.

"I don't know, but I have one suspect," announced Donnie. "I ran into Maribel on my way back to class. She was coming from that direction."

"Well, she does like art a lot," Jose commented. "Remember, she won that art contest last year around Halloween."

"Yeah, I remember," Donnie answered. "If she took the art supplies, then she must have stashed them in her locker right before I ran into her."

"Did you see anyone else when you went back for your lunch ticket?" Jose asked.

Donnie picked up a chicken strip and took a bite. He thought about the missing art supplies mystery for a moment. Then, he took a drink of milk before answering Jose.

"I did see Carl, the janitor. He was sweeping the hallway and helped me get into the classroom because Miss Gruber wasn't in there," Donnie replied. "But I don't think he'd want a bunch of kids' art supplies."

"Maybe not," Jose agreed. "But he might have seen someone else in the hallway that would. You should ask him."

Donnie planned to do just that next time he saw Carl. Maybe he'd seen another student near the classroom before Maribel ran by. Donnie couldn't wait to find out.

Donnie and Jose finished eating, cleaned up their trays, and ran outside for a short recess before their afternoon math lesson. The boys joined some other classmates, including Maribel, for a game of tag.

"You're it!" shouted Maribel as she tagged Donnie on the back. "No tag backs, either, Donnie."

"Wait, Maribel," said Donnie. "Did you know a bunch of art supplies are missing from Miss Gruber's class?"

"Oh, no. That's too bad," sympathized Maribel.

"Everything was there this morning," Donnie explained. "But they were missing when I went

back to class after we bumped into each other in the hallway."

"Hey, what are you saying Donnie?" Maribel's tone was serious now. "You think I took the supplies?"

Maribel didn't wait for an answer. She turned away from Donnie and joined another group of friends hanging around by the basketball hoop. Donnie felt bad. He didn't want Maribel to be mad at him. But he still thought she could have taken the supplies.

On the way back inside after recess, Donnie saw Carl emptying trash cans in the cafeteria. If he hurried, Donnie could ask Carl a few questions while everyone was heading back to class.

Carl saw Donnie approaching and gave him a friendly smile. "Hey there, kid. Did you ever find your lunch ticket?"

"Yep. Thanks for helping me," said Donnie.

"Did you see anyone else around there before helping me?"

"Why do you ask?" answered Carl.

"Well, a bunch of art supplies are missing from the classroom now, but they were all there this morning," Donnie explained.

"Art supplies, huh? That reminds me of something I need to do later," Carl suddenly seemed preoccupied with something else now, but Donnie wanted to get back to his questions. Carl continued on this new topic instead. "I have to drop off some toys and gifts for sick kids at the hospital later today. They're really great kids. They'd love visitors if you and your friends ever have a chance to stop by."

"I better get to class," Donnie interrupted. "Don't want to be late, but if you could just tell me if you saw anyone in the hallway earlier."

"Hmm, let me see," Carl paused for a moment. "Now that you mention it, there were two

45

older boys goofing off around there before you came by. I think they're sixth graders."

Donnie was excited at this new lead in the mystery. "Do you know who they were?"

"I don't know their names, kid," answered Carl. "There are too many of you to remember everyone's names, but I think they're brothers."

Donnie knew exactly who Carl was talking about. The Tyson brothers were non-identical twins in the sixth grade. They were always together, and they had a tendency to be mischievous. Donnie wasn't sure when he'd have a chance to talk to them about the missing art supplies. He'd be in class the rest of the afternoon until school ended. The Tyson brothers rode a different bus home than Donnie, and there usually wasn't time for anything else before getting on the bus. He might have to wait until morning to talk to the brothers in the cafeteria where everyone waited for the

teachers to call them into class.

Later that afternoon, Donnie paused to take a quick rest from the fractions he'd been dividing. Tapping his pencil against the desk, he glanced around the room wondering if anyone in his class had taken the art supplies. Miss Gruber had already made an announcement about the missing supplies after recess. No one confessed to taking them.

Donnie noticed Marissa and Carly passing notes to one another. They both loved drawing. Could they have taken the art supplies? Or was it Cody, the class clown, who liked pulling pranks? Maybe he thought it would be funny to make everyone think the supplies were stolen. It was the kind of thing he enjoyed doing.

SNAP! Donnie looked down at his pencil. After tapping it against the desk so long, the tip had snapped right off. Donnie got up and walked over to the pencil sharpener mounted on the wall near the windows. While staring out the window as he turned the crank around and around on the pencil sharpener, Donnie saw someone walking across the parking lot.

"Who is that?" Donnie wondered. He quickly realized it was Carl, and he was carrying a large bag. Donnie thought it looked like a garbage bag packed full of trash.

Carl popped open the trunk of his dark blue car. As he lifted up the large garbage bag to place it in the trunk, it spilled open. But it wasn't trash that fell out all over the pavement.

"Donnie," Miss Gruber's voice was soft, but stern. "What's taking you so long over there? Let's get back to work, please."

"Um, Miss Gruber," Donnie replied. "I think you might want to see this."

"What is it, Donnie?" asked Miss Gruber.

"I think I found the missing art supplies," answered Donnie.

The entire class jumped out of their seats and rushed to the windows to see for themselves. Sketch pads, colored pencils, paints, markers, glitter, stencils, and more were scattered across the pavement around the trunk of Carl's car.

"Class, please take your seats," Miss Gruber requested. "I'll be right back." She waited for everyone to sit back down at their desks before leaving.

As soon as Miss Gruber left the room, everyone jumped up and rushed back to the windows to watch what happened next. Carl was trying to quickly pick up all the different art supplies off the ground and stuff them back in the garbage bag.

"Hey, Donnie, everyone knows you took the art supplies out of the classroom," Cody said smugly. "What we don't know is why you gave them to the janitor."

"I didn't take anything, Cody," Donnie

argued. "Quit making stuff up!"

"Donnie, the art supply thief! Donnie, the art supply thief!" taunted Cody.

"Stop it, Cody," warned Donnie getting right up in Cody's face. "I didn't do anything, and you know it."

"What are you going to do, Donnie? Hit me?" laughed Cody.

"Hey everyone, Miss Gruber's outside now, and she's walking toward Carl," Jose interrupted.

"Let's open the windows," urged Donnie. "Maybe we can hear what they're saying."

"Miss Gruber sure was upset about the supplies being missing," said Cody. "I bet she's going to tell off that janitor real good. I wonder if she'll swear at him."

"Shh, Cody," whispered Donnie. "We can't hear what Miss Gruber is saying."

"Shh yourself, Donnie," Cody snapped back.

"Be quiet, Cody!" the entire class said in unison.

As the class finally quieted down, they could hear Miss Gruber asking Carl about the art supplies all over the ground. After talking for a few minutes, Carl finally admitted he had taken them from Miss Gruber's classroom. Donnie couldn't believe it. Why would Carl want some fourth-grade art supplies?

It was hard to hear everything Miss Gruber and Carl were saying, but the class heard enough to understand that Carl only wanted to donate them to the sick kids at the children's hospital. He thought that making art projects would bring smiles to their faces while being stuck in the hospital. Carl also told Miss Gruber he was going to replace the supplies later, but was heading to the hospital that day and didn't want to let the kids down by not bringing anything.

Donnie felt bad for the kids at the hospital. He remembered when he was in the hospital to have his tonsils removed. Suddenly, Donnie had a great idea.

"Hey, guys," Donnie said to the class. "Why don't we ask Miss Gruber if we can donate the art supplies to the kids in the hospital like Carl wanted to? Then, each of us can bring in one new supply to replace those. If we all bring in something, we'll still be able to make a class art project for the parents' open house next week. What do you guys think?"

"That sounds good," said Jose.

Other than Cody, who thought Carl should get in trouble for taking the supplies, the rest of the class agreed to donate the supplies. When Miss Gruber returned to the classroom, she was surprised to hear what the class had decided. But she thought it sounded like a nice idea.

At the end of the day, as everyone turned in their afternoon writing assignment and gathered their jackets and backpacks, Miss Gruber pulled Donnie aside to talk to him. He was a little worried about what she might say.

"Donnie, I just wanted to tell you I'm sorry I thought you took the art supplies," Miss Gruber apologized. "But as usual, you solved another mystery. Maybe you should think about being a detective when you grow up."

"Yeah, maybe," Donnie said. "I might just do that."

Donnie pictured himself solving crimes like the detectives he'd seen in movies. He thought that sounded pretty cool. But for now, he was just curious when his next mystery might pop up.

The Mysterious Lights

Warm summer air rushed over Donnie's hand as he dangled it out the car window. It was Friday, and his mom was letting him spend the entire weekend at Jose's house. They had it all planned out. He and Jose were going to sleep in the treehouse, go swimming, shoot hoops, and maybe even light some pre-Fourth of July fireworks with Jose's older brother Carlos. But Donnie didn't mention the fireworks to his mom. She probably wouldn't let him go if she knew.

Donnie was most excited about camping outside in the treehouse. Unlike his own neighborhood with houses neatly lined up one after another all the way down the block, Jose didn't have many neighbors. His family lived on the edge of town where it was quiet, and there wasn't much around except a few houses scattered about. The roads weren't paved, but made of dirt and gravel, and the school bus always bumped along as it neared Jose's house each day during the school year.

Even though it was pretty quiet out by Jose's house, there were still so many things to do. And Donnie thought it was one of the coolest places to hang out. Jose had a huge backyard that stretched back almost as long as a football field. The edge of his backyard was bordered by thick woods, which Donnie loved exploring anytime he could convince Jose to tag along.

Out in the treehouse in the quiet of night, you

could hear all sorts of sounds that Donnie didn't usually hear in his own backyard. Bull frogs croaking in the pond though the woods, crickets chirping, or an owl hooting off in the distance were the sounds that lulled Donnie and Jose to sleep in the treehouse.

"Alright, Donnie, we're here," said his mother. "You be good and listen to Jose's parents."

"Yes, Mom," said Donnie.

"I'll pick you up Sunday afternoon," said Donnie's mother. "Have fun. I'll miss you."

"Bye, Mom, miss you too," Donnie said while grabbing his backpack that had some extra clothes, his toothbrush, and a few other things inside. He gave his mom a quick wave goodbye, then ran down the long gravel driveway to Jose's house and disappeared inside.

Later that evening, Donnie and Jose headed out to the treehouse to get settled in for the night. They brought up sleeping bags and pillows and a couple flashlights. Jose also brought up his iPad in case they wanted to play games or watch videos. And he stashed a big bag of snacks up there too, so they wouldn't have to go back in the house if they got hungry. They were all set for the night. They had no reason to leave the treehouse, and Jose's parents had instructed them not to wander off. They could stay there or head back inside, but that was it. Leave it to Donnie, though, to soon find a reason to go exploring.

"Jose, do you see that?" asked Donnie.

"See what?" Jose replied.

"Look, over there by the woods," said Donnie pointing in that direction. "Those strange lights... you see them?"

"Yeah, I see them now," said Jose. "What are they?"

"I don't know, but they look cool," answered Donnie. "You want to go take a closer look?"

"No way, Donnie. I'm not going anywhere near those woods at night," insisted Jose. "Plus, my parents will get mad if they find out we left the treehouse."

"Please, Jose," pleaded Donnie. "We'll just walk to the edge of your yard for a closer look. We don't have to go in the woods. Come on, please?"

Jose hesitated, but finally agreed if Donnie promised they would only take a quick look and come right back.

The two boys grabbed their flashlights and climbed down from the treehouse. As they walked toward the woods, they saw flashes of green and blue lights poking through the trees ahead.

"I wonder where those lights are coming from," said Donnie.

"Maybe they're ghosts," suggested Jose.

"They're not ghosts, Jose," Donnie said with

confidence. "There's no such thing as ghosts."

"How do you know? There could be," answered Jose.

"I don't think so," said Donnie.

"Maybe it's La Llorona," Jose said.

"Lah-your what?" Donnie asked, a bit confused.

"Lah-your-own-ah," pronounced Jose slowly.

"What's that?" asked Donnie.

"It's a crying lady who lost her kids," explained Jose. "My brother told me about her. She lived in a small village, and one night when she was washing her clothes in the river, her kids wandered off, and she couldn't find them. Now, she wanders around crying at night looking for her lost children. Legend has it that she'll take any kids she finds, so it's best not to be out wandering around at night."

"Yeah, right," said Donnie. "Your brother was

probably just trying to scare you."

"I don't think so, Donnie. My grandmother told him that story. She grew up in the same village La Llorona came from," insisted Jose.

"Well, I don't know about all that," said Donnie. "But I'm sure those lights in the woods are not the crying lady. And just to prove it, I think we should go in there."

"Go in the woods? Are you crazy?" said Jose.

"Well, I'm going," Donnie said. "You can wait here by yourself if you want."

Donnie made his way a few feet into the dark woods. Jose reluctantly followed. He didn't want to be left behind by himself. It was quiet, except for the occasional croak of a bull frog.

"Look, Jose!" shouted Donnie excitedly. "There are the lights again. Let's go check it out."

"This is not a good idea," warned Jose. "Let's

just turn around and get out of here. La Llorona might get us. Plus, I'm hungry."

"We'll go back in a minute," promised Donnie. "I just want to see what's making those bright lights."

It was no use trying to convince Donnie to head back to the safety of the treehouse. Once he had his mind set on doing something, he was determined to see it through. This was especially true whenever there was a mystery to solve.

The two soon-to-be fifth graders slowly made their way a little farther into the woods. Most of the time, the lights were green and blue, but occasionally there were red lights as well. Sometimes, the colorful lights could be seen for several minutes at a time. And other times, they disappeared almost as quickly as they appeared.

As Donnie and Jose continued heading

farther into the woods, the mysterious lights kept getting brighter. Donnie knew they must be getting closer, and he was determined to discover where the lights were coming from. He didn't want to head back to the treehouse without knowing.

The two boys were almost to the other side of the woods. Through the last few trees they could see a clearing that looked like a big open yard without trees. Then, they saw two shadowy figures across the clearing.

"Hey, who's over there?!" shouted one of the dark figures in the clearing. The other figure started heading toward the woods.

"Oh, no! They saw us," Donnie said frantically.

"Run!" yelled Jose.

The boys turned around and sprinted back through the woods. They could hear the snap of sticks being stepped on and broken as one of the dark figures chased them through the

woods. Donnie and Jose had never run so fast in their lives. The other side of the woods that spilled out to the edge of Jose's yard couldn't come soon enough. Right about then, Donnie thought that maybe he should have listened to Jose and stayed in the treehouse.

The edge of the woods was finally in sight. The boys were almost back in Jose's yard. Just as they were about to pass through the last row of trees and escape the spooky woods, Jose yelled out for help. Donnie turned around to see that his best friend had been caught by the strange figure chasing them. Donnie clicked on his flashlight and shined it in the stranger's face. To his surprise, it wasn't a stranger at all!

"Carlos, is that you?" Donnie asked the older figure holding onto Jose.

"Yes, it's me," Jose's older brother reassured the boys. "What are you two doing running around out here? Mom and Dad won't be happy about this."

"Please don't tell them, Carlos," begged Jose. "Then they'll make us go inside, and we won't be able to camp out in the treehouse anymore."

"Relax, little brother. I'm not going to tell them," said Carlos. "But what were you guys doing in the woods?"

"We saw some crazy lights flashing on and off, and we wanted to see what they were," explained Donnie.

"I told him it was probably La Llorona," said Jose. "But it could be aliens too."

"Oh, Jose. You have quite the imagination, don't you?" teased Carlos.

Carlos laughed and even Donnie let out a little giggle. Jose didn't appreciate being teased or laughed at. He insisted the lights could at least be ghosts or aliens, if they weren't coming from La Llorona.

"Okay, guys," said Carlos. "This was supposed to be a surprise for the Fourth of July, but I'll tell you what those lights are all about if you both promise not to tell anyone else."

Donnie and Jose listened closely as Carlos explained that the mysterious lights were part of a laser light show one of his friends was planning for Fourth of July. The lights were going to be turned on during the fireworks display. There would be lights everywhere from the fireworks in the sky to the laser lights on the ground. "It's going to be epic," said Carlos excitedly.

"That's pretty cool, but I still think it would be cooler if those lights were coming from La Llorona," said Jose.

"You know what, Jose? Me too," said Donnie. "I kind of like that story about the crying lady now."

"Well, you're in luck then," said Carlos.

"Because I know all about her. Why don't I walk you guys back to the treehouse and tell you all about the legend of La Llorona?"

With the mystery of the mysterious lights solved, Donnie could just relax and enjoy the rest of the campout in the treehouse. And he was looking forward to the story of La Llorona. But in the back of his mind, he couldn't help but wonder what mystery he'd solve next.